STRIKE BACK

A NOVELLA IN THE ECHO PLATOON SERIES

MARLISS MELTON

A NOTICE TO THE READER/LIMIT OF LIABILITY/DISCLAIMER OF WARRANTY:

James-York Press
Williamsburg, Virginia

Edited by Sydney J. Baily
Cover Design by Dar Dixon
Book Layout by BB eBooks

ISBN-13: 978-1-938732-27-0

DEDICATION

I dedicate this story to readers who have read *all* of my books. This may be the last Marliss Melton title, at least for a while. Please look for my Inspired Warriors series to be written by my alter ego, Rebecca Hartt. The first book, BACK TO EDEN, is a fresh take on my first SEAL Team Twelve book, FORGET ME NOT. If you have loved my stories, you may wish to preorder BACK TO EDEN on Amazon. Bless you for your loyalty!

ACKNOWLEDGMENTS

What can I say? Penny Doyle, Deborah Whaley, and Jan Albertie—you three ladies are a treasure. I have valued your keen eyes and your dedication like a secret treasure. From the bottom of my heart, I thank you for being my beta readers.

CHAPTER ONE

A T TWILIGHT, HILARY Alcorn backed from her parking space at the National Counterterrorism Center where she worked and headed for the exit. The levered arm in front of the gate house lifted at her approach. Slowing as she passed the gate, she blew a kiss at Harold, who waved her through. Easing onto the curved road that took her to the stoplight, Hilary braked to await a green arrow. A pair of rectangular headlights drew up behind her, inspiring a sense of déjà vu as she eyed them through her rearview mirror.

Hadn't a car with identical headlights pulled up super-close to her bumper last night, too? Narrowing blue-green eyes behind her teal-framed lenses, Hilary scrutinized what appeared to be a man driving the dark sedan.

Maybe he was following her.

Pfft. Sure, he is!

Scoffing at her imagination, she punched the accelerator as a green arrow pierced the darkness. Plenty of cars were leaving the Liberty Crossing Intelligence Campus at that time of night. Like her, the driver behind had probably worked late to avoid the rush-hour traffic. In Northern Virginia, just miles from Washington, D.C., Hilary's ten-minute drive home could turn into an hour-long commute through hell if she left work too early.

That was her excuse, anyway, for hanging around the office until seven most evenings. The truth was she didn't want to be alone in her apartment with just her cat for companionship. And ever since a certain Navy SEAL had walked out of her life, she'd had no desire to go out looking for company elsewhere. That left the office, where at least she had company.

Heaving a tortured sigh, Hilary zipped up the ramp to merge onto the beltway. Her volcanic-orange Mini Cooper with its turbo-charged engine outstripped the sedan behind her. Too bad, she thought. Life would be more interesting if she *were* being followed. Maybe if something awful happened to her, Stuart Rudolph would take an interest in her again. In her loneliness, she entertained that thought for a tortured moment.

He'd come into her life when she was still working for her friend and private investigator, Juliet Rhodes. Finding a spy from the Cold War era based on his composite alone had stymied both Hilary and Juliet, so they'd called on a friend of Juliet's Navy SEAL boyfriend, a man so good at finding information online his SEAL buddies called him Hack.

Before Hilary had met Stuart, she had known plenty of men—many of them in the Biblical sense. After meeting him, she could care less about other men. She wasn't sure what he had done to her, but she wasn't the same flamboyant woman that she used to be. She no longer craved male attention. The only thing she craved was Stuart, who'd walked away over a stupid misunderstanding.

"Damn him." A familiar wave of longing rolled through her. When would this never-ending craving for him cease? If he'd felt half as much for her as she felt for him, he wouldn't have allowed a small misunderstanding to tear them apart. They'd still be together, probably going to the latest *Star Wars* movie playing at the theater this weekend.

Oh, God. Had that whimper of regret come from her own lips?

"I have to move on," Hilary stated as she slowed at a stoplight just a block from her apartment. A glance into her rearview mirror made her eyes widen. That same American-made sedan was pulling up behind her again. Her stomach lurched with sudden dread. She *was* being followed!

Or was her new job at the National Counter-terrorism Center making her paranoid?

The light blipped green, and Hilary floored the accelerator, tearing up the last two streets to her apartment complex where she nosed her Mini into her designated parking space. Just as she killed her engine, the rectangular headlights swung into view, causing her pulse to spike. She reached for her cell phone as it rolled into a space three cars over.

Peering through the windows of the cars in between, she glimpsed a pair of broad shoulders and a head of dark hair as the driver exited his vehicle. Without so much as a glance in her direction, he struck out for her building, walking under a streetlamp as he did so.

Recognition flooded her with relief, followed immediately by a sense of anticlimax. It was only her neighbor from the apartment directly under hers, the MIT graduate who'd moved to Fairfax the previous summer looking for a job. She'd chatted with him at the Fourth-of-July pool party at the clubhouse back when she made it a point to introduce herself to all single men.

Annoyed and feeling somewhat foolish, Hilary pushed out of her vehicle to follow her neighbor's example. As she climbed the stairs to her third-story apartment, she spied the former grad student standing at his door on the second floor, inserting his key into his lock. He looked over at the sound of her footsteps and smiled. The flash of straight white teeth framed by a dark goatee sparked an unexpected response. Hilary's step slowed.

"Hey," he called, and his deep, baritone voice tickled something inside her. "I think we work in the same location. I followed you home."

His name surfaced suddenly. "Elias, right?"

Eschewing the stairs that conveyed her to her own apartment, she approached him with a tentative smile.

"Yes." He grinned with delight that she'd remembered his name. "You're Hilary."

"Yes, I am."

Dark, deep-set eyes considered her with interest as he turned his solid, stocky body to face her fully. Self-awareness elevated Hilary's heart rate. After months of feeling unwanted, it came as a relief to pull her shoulders back, lift her chin, and let him look.

"Wow, you look different," he said.

"Better or worse?" she asked with private concern.

"Well, you've lost some weight, not that you were chubby before—I like women with curves so it doesn't matter to me one way or another."

He was rambling. *I make him ramble,* she thought, giving herself a mental high five.

Embracing her feminine power, Hilary sashayed closer.

"I've been walking more," she admitted, which was true. Every morning she zipped through the entire park across the street, asking herself with every step why Stu wasn't in her life anymore.

"Your hair's longer," he added.

She'd given up cutting it short and dying it ruby red. Now, it fell to her shoulders in a tumble of golden-brown curls. With the new hairstyle came a new wardrobe. She had laid aside the neon colors and eye-catching patterns that she used to wear. What was the point of dressing like a canary when she didn't feel like singing? Besides, she'd known for years it was an over-the-top wardrobe designed to get attention.

"So, where do you work?" she asked, shifting the focus off herself.

"I got a job with the Intelligence Advanced Research Projects Activity—IARPA." He nodded enthusiastically, clearly pleased with his accomplishment. "Yeah, it keeps me really busy."

"Right out of grad school. That's incredible," she praised. "You work right next door to me."

"You're at NCTC?"

"Yep." As a rule, she didn't tell just anyone about her current job, but Elias obviously had clearance himself, so no harm, no foul.

"We should get together some time and compare notes," he suggested.

Her pulse skipped at the offer. Was he asking her out or just being polite? After all, he had to be five years younger than she was. Stu was two years younger, and that hadn't been an issue, but five years?

On the other hand, he resembled Stu with his swarthy coloring. He wasn't as tall, of course, or as physically fit, but then she tended to carry a little extra weight herself.

"Maybe we should," she said, unable to make up her mind.

The gleam that flashed in his eyes informed her he was definitely interested.

So, why not? she asked herself. She didn't expect to connect over *Star Wars* or *Harry Potter*, the way she and Stu had. Not that everything about their relationship had been juvenile. They'd also shared deep conversations about their childhoods and how it had shaped them as adults. And, of course, there were those incredible kisses that promised the sweetest of lovemaking, but they'd never gotten that far. What a waste! Oh, this was pointless. Elias would never fill—

"How about tonight?" he asked unexpectedly.

She deliberated the prospect of a respite from her loneliness and nearly accepted. Nearly.

"Sorry, I've got a friend coming over." The white lie found its way to her lips. "Maybe some other time?"

"A guy friend?"

The question gave her pause—jealous much? Maybe he simply wanted a feel for her availability.

"No. I'm not seeing anyone right now." Saying the words out loud made them all the more painful.

Elias seemed to relax. His gaze slid over her one more time. "Well, then, let's talk again some time."

Loath to let a prospective date slip by away entirely, she asked, "Do you have a Facebook page?"

"Umm, sure." He paused as if trying to remember something. "Search for Elias Malki." He spelled his last name. "I'm the only one."

"I'll send you a friend request," she promised.

"Great. I'll look for it."

With a decisive nod, she pivoted toward the stairs, aware, as she climbed them, of his gaze sliding toward the hem of her skirt to her shapely calves. Sighing again, she imagined how he would have appreciated her old style of sheer thigh-highs and a garter belt. She wore practical pantyhose now, at least until the weather warmed.

Pantyhose or not, Elias's regard managed to make her feel sexy. For months now, she'd done nothing but mope in the wake of Stuart Rudolph's abrupt abandonment. Recalling the way Stu had caressed her, the depth of their cerebral connection, she still ached for him. No other man could ever fill the spaces in her heart and head that he had filled. But she had to move on. At least she responded physically to Elias Malki.

It's a start, she told herself.

STUART RUDOLPH KEPT multiple browsers open on all six monitors positioned around his U-shaped desk. Sitting at his desk was like being on the bridge of the fictional starship *Enterprise*. The Universe lay at his fingertips. Collecting actionable threat data, he jumped from dating sites to chat rooms to satellite imaging, all the while keeping tabs on extremists.

Under the alias Oscar Atta, Stu advertised himself as a vocal proponent of the Islamic State of Iraq and the Levant. In this cyber world, he had become an extremist of the worst sort, expressing his desire to expand the caliphate by beheading, crucifying, and enslaving nonbelievers.

His white-hat hacking skills had become legend, making him the perfect liaison between Special Operations Command and Ghost Security Group, a counterterrorism organization that took on digital *jihad*. As both a SEAL and a member of GSG, Stu battled the war on terror both on the ground and online.

He had taken on the GSG job in the last few months to keep himself busy. Or rather, even busier. With both his body and his brain taxed to the extreme, he didn't have time to think about Hilary Alcorn, the one woman he'd loved and lost because he'd failed her.

Not only was Hilary affectionate and sexy, but they spoke the same languages. Whether he talked about the Dark Net or in Klingon, she understood what he said—not that he talked a lot. As a kid, he'd been diagnosed with Asperger's, though that term had fallen out of favor in recent years. At work, no one realized he was on the autism spectrum. His affinity for computers merely enhanced his physical athleticism. His differences were only apparent in social situations—especially when women were involved.

Hilary hadn't even seemed to notice. From their very first meeting, she'd accepted him without a shred of judgment. Her eyes had shone with admiration, easing his awkwardness. He had helped her on a case last fall, tracking down an East German spy still on the lam from the Cold War era and living in the U.S. Who knew what else they could have accomplished if Stu hadn't made Hilary a promise and then promptly broken it, telling his teammate Justin a secret he wasn't supposed to share.

Clearly, Stu had never deserved Hilary.

She claimed to forgive him—over and over in texts and in voicemails. What's more, he believed her. But he couldn't forgive himself. Period. Instead, he'd got himself a new phone number and blocked her from his world. Unfortunately, as he well understood about himself, there were no shades of gray in his coloring box, only black and white. He'd given her his word; he'd broken it. He didn't deserve Hilary Alcorn's love. Not even if she wanted to give it to him.

If only he could sever his memories of her as easily as he could change his phone number. Instead, those memories stubbornly persisted, along with a nameless yearning and a propensity to daydream that got in the way of his work—like right now. *Damn it!*

Catching himself off task—*again*—Stu focused once more on the monitors before him. All over the world, terrorists were launching cyber-attacks against the DoD, hacking into intelligence systems, and undermining financial, military, and transportation infrastructures. He couldn't afford to be distracted by a memory that wouldn't go away.

The realization made him pause. It had been, what, five months now since he'd broken it off with Hilary? Yet he still thought of her, at least once an hour. That kind of interference was like having a virus plaguing a computer's operational system. In layman's terms, which weren't technically accurate, viruses required a patch. Maybe that was what he needed—to put a patch on his relationship with Hilary.

The thought took hold and wouldn't leave him.

His gaze slid thoughtfully to the Facebook profile of his alias, Oscar Atta. Hilary would immediately recognize the name Oscar, especially when paired with the avatar of Stu's Maine Coon cat. Perhaps if she accepted his friend request, and he knew what was going on with her, he would have a connection that satisfied the hankering inside of him. Then he could focus on his work again.

Why not? If it didn't work, he'd just unfriend her. Directing his mouse to the appropriate screen, he reached out through cyberspace to close the gap between them.

CHAPTER TWO

S HEDDING HER WORK attire, Hilary donned turquoise pajamas dotted with lime-green polka dots and, postponing her dinner, settled onto her sofa with Mitzie, her orange-and-white calico. Only when the feline rumbled with contentment from a good dose of loving did Hilary set Mitzie aside and pull her Mac Book Pro onto her lap. For the past few months, this was how she had done her socializing.

Tonight, she would send Elias Malki a Facebook friend request and take one brave step toward getting over Stu.

A brief search turned up Elias's profile almost immediately. She perused it, noting how he'd filled his home page with lighthearted postings and pictures of himself enjoying moments with friends. Wow. He had a lot of friends, several from college and even more with foreign names. She wondered what his heritage was—Syrian maybe? His parents must have been immigrants. She clicked the Add Friend button then waited on pins and needles for him to accept.

To her delight, the people icon at the top of her page lit up. She clicked on it only to blink in confusion. Someone named Oscar Atta had requested that she befriend *him*.

Who the hell was Oscar Atta?

Opening the man's profile, she gasped in recognition of the gorgeous Maine Coon cat in the picture. Stu's cat. Oh, my God, Stu had just sent her a friend request! Her heart took off at an Indie-500 gallop.

Yes! Yes! Yes! She accepted his friend request at once, swallowed against a dry mouth, then hungrily absorbed everything she could on Oscar Atta's profile.

"Huh." Her eyebrows pulled together as she tried to make sense of the posts. They spewed with anti-American rhetoric. His photos all depicted violence. Like Elias, he had hundreds of friends, most of them foreign, which was weird, since Stu didn't have any friends she knew outside of his SEAL team brothers.

His profile made no sense. Stu was a patriot. Day in and day out, he laid his life on the line for his country, so what was this picture of the American flag on fire? And what about his one mocking his Commander-in-Chief? Here was a link to a site called How to Make a Homemade Bomb.

"What the—?"

An answer burst over her suddenly. Oh, of course. This Facebook page was a means of attracting extremists. It wasn't really Stu's profile, anyway; it was Oscar's, his crazy cat's.

Oh, dear. Hilary didn't relish her name showing up for all of Oscar's radical friends to see. But that was okay for now. At least, he'd reached out to her. After he'd changed his phone number, she was certain she would never hear from him again.

Ding! Hilary's heart leaped as Messenger notified her of someone attempting to chat. Stu? No. Disappointment pinched her. Just Elias. He'd accepted her friend request and promptly sent her a message.

Hi, Hilary. Is your friend there yet?

Concerned he'd be knocking on her door if she didn't lie, she typed back: *Hi. No, but she'll be here any minute. What about you? Don't you have plans?* It was Friday night.

Not yet.

His reply seemed to hint that could change depending on her.

She heaved a heavy sigh. *You've got a lot of friends on FB. Maybe you could hit up one of them.*

I'm a people person.

He'd completely ignored her suggestion.

Hey, you want to do something fun tomorrow? he asked before she thought of what to type back.

Like what? In truth, she wanted to stop this conversation with Elias so she could focus on what to say to Stu in a message.

There's a Federal Identity Forum & Exposition at the Homeland Security Conference in downtown D.C. Want to go?

The Expo was right up her alley. She had seen a flyer at work advertising the array of exhibits from encryption to facial recognition to cybersecurity solutions and biometric authentication, and she'd been thinking of going by herself. Might as well have company.

Sure, she typed. A work-related outing wouldn't count as a date because she couldn't even think about dating Elias if Stu was still an option.

For the next few minutes, they went back and forth on the best way to get downtown, then settled on taking the metro. Hilary would knock on Elias's apartment door at 11 a.m. Then they'd drive to the nearest metro station, leaving the car there.

Oh, my friend's here now, she added, suddenly ready to end their back-and-forth.

Uh, okay. See you tomorrow, Elias replied.

She went straight to messaging Stu. *Are you there?* Her heart beat at the base of her throat as she waited for an answer.

Always.

That single word of devotion utterly melted her. Then she considered what he'd probably meant—that he was always on his laptop.

How've you been? she dared to ask.

It took him an inordinately long time to write back. *So-so. You?*

Might as well be honest, she thought with a shrug. *Terrible.*

Her eyes widened at the full sentence that came from him next. *I'm going to be working up in D.C. the first part of next week.*

Oh, my God. He was going to be close to her, instead of four hours away in Virginia Beach.

Without hesitating, without thinking of how much it would hurt when he turned her down, she typed: *Can we meet?* Her mouth turned dry as she waited to be rebuffed again.

And waited. And waited.

At last he typed back, *OK.*

The one little word had her closing her eyes in relief. *When? Where?* Afraid to say too much, she kept her questions to a minimum.

I'll send you a message on Sunday when I know my schedule better.

Anxiety gripped her. What if he changed his mind in the next thirty-six hours? She'd be devastated all over again, but she didn't dare to push for commitment. Even so, she could let him know she was going to be waiting.

Don't forget, she typed, glad he couldn't discern the pleading tone she would use if she'd said the words aloud.

I won't.

She bit her lower lip to keep her chin from wobbling. Tears filled her eyes, blurring the words she typed. Again, she might as well be honest: *Can't wait to see you.*

Trembling with hope, she waited for him to say *Me neither.* Instead he went quiet. The sound of her own breath, flowing quickly in and out of her lungs was all she heard, besides the purring of her cat. Hoping she hadn't scared him off by coming on too strong, she heaved a deep, anguished sigh. At least he had said that he wouldn't forget.

One thing she knew for sure about Stu, his word was his bond. That damned honorable bond had destroyed them the last time.

Now she had a way to contact him, she realized.

With a small, hopeful smile, she put aside her laptop and got up to make dinner.

CHAPTER THREE

"OH, CRAP, I forgot my access card," Elias lamented, even as he patted down his pockets for his government ID. They stood in a fast-moving line for their ticket into the exhibit hall.

Hilary's gaze swung to the cost of admission, posted on the large placard hanging by the ticket window.

"Anyone who's not a student or a government employee has to pay $150!" she relayed with dismay.

"Wait, students are free?" Elias's grin brought a dimple out of his goatee. He whipped out a laminated card and showed it to her. "Look what I still have."

On their metro ride into D.C. that morning,

he'd proven to be a cheerful and charming companion. Getting through the day so tomorrow would come faster wouldn't be so difficult, Hilary had realized, grateful for the distraction.

Peering dubiously at the photo on Elias's ID from MIT, she wondered, "You think that's still valid?" He looked like a kid without the beard.

"I don't think they'll check," he said on a confident whisper.

Sure enough, the person doling out tickets glanced only cursorily at their IDs before handing over two passes. With a conspiring wink, Elias escorted her past the trio of security guards and into the convention center.

A buzz of intellectual excitement filled the enormous indoor arena. The entire space had been partitioned into grids to accommodate the many exhibits. Colorful banners advertised state-of-the-art iris recognition, mobile solutions, and voice verification. Earnest-faced individuals milled before the displays. Hilary's gaze went straight to a head of prematurely silver hair.

"Oh, there's my boss," she said. In lieu of his usual suit, Isaac Calhoun wore a flannel shirt and carried a baby resting on his left shoulder.

"Who? Where?" Elias asked, and she pointed Calhoun out to him.

His eyebrows rose with interest. "You'll have to tell me about him later." He turned his attention eagerly to the displays. "Where should we start?"

She gestured to the nearest booth. "How about here? Then we'll move clockwise," she suggested.

"Works for me."

As they bellied up to the first table, Elias reached for Hilary's hand. At the feel of his warm fingers encasing hers, her nerves jangled. While it wasn't at all unpleasant, it was unfamiliar. She immediately thought of Stu and, by the second booth, pretending to reach for something, she managed to free herself without rebuffing Elias entirely.

To her relief, he didn't try holding her hand again. They moved on, chatting amiably about the options on display and their potential applications.

Minutes later, they rounded the end of the first aisle, and Hilary's gaze snagged on the dark headed man standing several inches above anyone around him. Poignant desire lanced her as she thought of Stu again. Then the man turned in her direction, and the air in her throat reversed direction. My, God, it *was* Stu!

He was here. At the Expo!

She must have swayed in shock because Elias grabbed her arm.

"You okay?"

Just then, Stu started toward them. Her gaze locked with his, and his stride faltered. Delayed recognition—after all, her hair was no longer ruby red—gave way to an expressionless mask as he noted her arm in Elias's grasp.

Pulling her elbow free, Hilary deliberately closed the space between them. With a helpless smile, she soaked in the sight of him. Had he always been so tall, so broad, so striking?

"Stu," she exclaimed, "you're here at the Expo. I didn't know you'd be here. I mean, how could I know you'd be here?" She wanted to tear her arm off and stuff it in her own mouth to stop from talking. Instead, she finally clamped her lips closed.

Saying nothing in response, his gaze seemed to catalogue her many transformations.

"Yeah, I look different, huh?" She lifted a hand to her golden-brown curls.

Still, Stu didn't answer. His gaze shifted to encompass Elias, who had joined them, and she added, "This is Elias Malki, my neighbor."

It's not a date, she wanted to add, but Elias might take offense.

"How are you?" Elias jutted out a hand and beamed at Stu, who hesitated, then clasped his hand briefly.

"Elias, this is Stuart Rudolph. He's uh—" she cut herself off recalling it wasn't wise to reveal Stu's actual occupation as a SEAL.

"Ghost Security Group," Stu murmured his first words into the silence.

Wait, what?

Elias's mouth popped open. "No shit." His eyes rounded as he looked Stu up and down. "I always pictured those guys as out-of-shape Millennials—like me," he added with a self-deprecating chuckle and a pat on his slight paunch.

"You're not out of shape," Hilary said to fill a second awkward silence. Out the corner of her eye she considered Stu, wondering if he'd made up a lie on the fly to cover up what he really did.

"Well, thanks." Elias elbowed her in a familiar manner.

I'm not with him. She wished she could just say the words out loud. Stu was staring at them hard. She would message him as soon as she slipped into the restroom, she decided.

All at once a lovely brunette, older than any of them but in remarkable shape, appeared at Stu's elbow. Jealousy nipped at Hilary as the woman's cool green eyes drifted over her before she spared both her and Elias a curt nod.

"Shall we go?" she said to Stu brusquely.

"Yeah." Tearing his gaze from Hilary, Stu started turning away.

Not even a word of goodbye after all this time? She knew she should be hurt and angry at his treatment of her, but there was still the promise of tomorrow. He said he'd contact her on Sunday.

"I'll see you," Hilary called out, wishing she hadn't sounded like a desperate schoolgirl.

With the barest nod of acknowledgment, he walked off with Madam Fitness. The woman's long, chocolate brown ponytail swished behind her like a horse's well-groomed tail as they rapidly retreated.

What the hell was that about?

Out of her peripheral vision, Hilary could

tell Elias was staring at her. "Wow, you know a Ghost." He sounded thoroughly impressed.

Hilary had never heard that term before. "Not that well," she said with a careless shrug. *Not nearly as badly as I want to know him,* she added silently.

"He doesn't talk much, does he?"

"Apparently not."

Her breezy tone hinted for him to drop the subject. But he didn't.

"You're going to see him again?"

"Who knows." Not if Stu forgot to message her tomorrow.

"Like, personally, or…?"

Turning her head, she sent Elias a pointed smile. "Who knows?" she repeated.

He finally got the hint to mind his own business.

"Look," he said, pretending interest in the display on signature verification software. "Let's check this out."

CHAPTER FOUR

ENTERING HIS HOTEL suite, Stu set the chain then went straight to the desk, pulling his laptop from his backpack.

Hilary—her face, her hair, her smile, her eyes, her essence—popped into his head as it had done a million times since running into her earlier. Blinking, he ran a hand over his tired eyes and tried to focus.

His meeting with the director of Ghost Security Group had lasted well into the evening. As he'd sat across from the man, he'd found himself thinking about the comment made by Hilary's friend at the Expo. *I always pictured those guys as out-of-shape Millennials—like me.*

Elias Malki's comment hadn't been that far off the mark. GSG's director was a Brit with a potbelly and facial hair, and he wasn't a day older than Stu.

Their meeting had touched on GSG's objectives: Get as many Islamic State social media accounts taken offline as possible; report accounts and links owned by ISIL to service providers; and share data identifying accounts and servers with the analyst who contributed to the Congressional Task Force on Terrorism and Unconventional Warfare. That analyst was Lucy Atwater, the woman who'd accompanied Stu to the Expo. She also worked for the CIA, and her husband was a former SEAL.

No technology had been permitted in the space where they'd met, so Stu had memorized what he needed to know. He would lose an extra hour of sleep right now typing up details and directives he didn't want to forget.

Before he did that, though, he wanted to know more about Elias Malki. Hilary had sent him a message via Facebook that Elias was her neighbor, not a date. Given the way she used to throw herself at strangers, Stu wasn't sure he quite believed her. How convenient to have a lover living right there in the same building as her, rather than hours away.

Jealousy had gnawed at him all day.

While accessing a secure server, Stu pictured again how Hilary had looked at the Expo. His stomach lurched like it did on a turbulent helo ride. Had she always been so lovely?

In lieu of short, red hair, a tumble of golden brown curls framed her face, making her eyes look even bigger behind the lenses of her glasses. Instead of some brightly colored outfit, she'd worn jeans and a pale pink sweater that matched the bloom in her cheeks. The embroidered flowers on her ankle boots were her only visible accessory—no more dazzling rings or gaudy earrings.

In fact, she had looked so normal and cute that he'd nearly looked past her without recognizing her. And then the realization of who was standing there looking at him had hit him like an IED exploding right under his feet.

The experience had jolted him, he had to admit. The sight of her after all these months had certainly set back his social skills about ten years, as he recalled how little he'd said. Then he'd had an epiphany.

Maybe, with her change from glitter girl to a more pedantic version, a guy like him stood a chance with her.

The way she'd dressed before—all bright and garish, dripping with costume jewelry—he had never been able to picture himself with her. That was on him. Though when they were alone, it had been all about their intense connection. How she'd dressed hadn't mattered. He would never have suggested she change herself, but since she already had, if he was honest, the way she looked today . . . yeah, she was more approachable, more on his level. But he might be too late. Her sweet, simple looks would attract any number of guys, and Elias Malki might have stolen her away already. She might have Facebook messaged Stu just to make him feel better about meeting his replacement.

Elias Malki. An unusual name. Why did it sound so familiar? Stu was certain he had seen or heard it somewhere.

Inputting the name into a Google search, he studied the results—student publications and a Facebook profile. Stu opened the latter through his own Facebook account then blinked in surprise at the checked FRIENDS box. What the hell?

He—or, rather, Oscar Atta—and Elias Malki

were friends already. No wonder that name sounded so familiar.

Stu went to check if they had any friends in common—and, yes, they did: Sayid Zafrani, Tarek Haik, and Hilary Alcorn.

Holy shit. Sitting forward, Stu stared at the avatars of the two men first. Both were well known to Ghost Security Group as suspected ISIL supporters living in Chicago. Seeing Hilary's name listed under theirs literally tied Stu's stomach into knots. Why the hell was a friend of Hilary's also friends with those two men?

A reasonable explanation sprang to mind. Maybe Elias was a terrorist hunter like Stu. He could be working for the FBI or something.

The only other explanation drove needles of alarm into Stu's scalp. Elias might also be a proponent for the Islamic State. After all, the greatest threat to US security came from insiders, especially ones like this guy, highly educated with ties to the Middle East.

Tearing through Elias's profile, Stu searched for clues suggesting the man's allegiance. He had dozens of friends with exotic surnames. Most of them, Stu determined, were young and living in Ohio. Most of them had attended MIT like Elias had.

Stu sat back in his chair and frowned. Now Hilary was a common friend. By sending her a friend request, Stu had unwittingly pulled her into his shadowy underworld.

There was only one sure way to keep her out of it. Returning to his own profile, he accessed his list of friends and promptly unfriended her.

No harm, no foul, he assured himself. The only way Elias Malki would have noticed Hilary was once friends with Oscar Atta was if he'd been on Facebook in the last twenty-four hours and monitored who Oscar's friends were.

Not likely, right?

Hilary was safer this way, Stu assured himself. Yet he was left feeling keenly isolated, knowing Hilary couldn't chat with him via Messenger anymore.

No worries. Tomorrow, he would call her directly, thus giving her his new phone number. After that, they could text whenever they wanted. He was ready for that. Seeing her today had given him that push he needed to reopen their lines of communication. If only he could shake the worry that he'd lost her to another man.

CHAPTER FIVE

"**S**O, HOW DO you know Oscar Atta?"

The unexpected question, volleyed across the small table between them, wrested Hilary's attention from the couple bickering next to them. She met Elias's intent regard with a blank expression, thoughts shifting into warp speed as she analyzed his inquiry.

In a bid to buy more time, she picked up the Cosmo cocktail she had just ordered and took a slow sip.

In lieu of going home after the Expo, Elias had talked her into touring a museum then catching dinner afterward. Then, coincidentally, he'd chosen a trendy restaurant in Chinatown, right next to the hole-in-the-wall restaurant she and Stu had visited six months before.

Elias's question had thrown her off balance. How did he even know Oscar Atta's name?

"I don't recognize that name," she lied, setting her drink down and maintaining direct eye contact.

His thick eyebrows drew together as his gaze bore into hers. "Really?"

"What makes you think I know him?" Hilary continued on a casual note.

"Well, when I answered your friend request last night, it said we had a friend in common named Oscar Atta."

"Huh." Hilary clung to her assertion. "I couldn't tell you who that is. You know Facebook. We all have a lot of *friends* who are really strangers."

"Here, I'll show you." Elias pulled his phone out, presumably to access his list of friends on Facebook.

Watching him, Hilary's mind raced ahead of her fast-beating heart. Why on earth would Elias be friends with Oscar Atta? She reached for a coconut-encrusted shrimp and munched it to cover up her consternation.

"Hmm." Elias frowned at his phone, then shook his head and shrugged. "Well, my mistake," he said, placing it back on the table. "If you were friends with him, you're not anymore."

What? Concern usurped her initial relief. She wasn't Stu's friend anymore? "Must have been a fluke," she murmured. "I've never heard of Oscar Atta."

"Well, I hope so," Elias replied. Leaning closer, he pitched his voice low and said, "The man is a known dissident. You'll want to stay away from him if you don't want to lose your clearance."

"Wait," she said, "then why are you friends with him?"

He sent her a condescending grimace. "It's my job," he told her simply.

His assertion relieved her suspicions immediately. Now she was dying to know two things at once. What exactly did Elias do with Intelligence Advanced Research Projects Activity? And why had Stu unfriended her? Hadn't he seen the message she'd sent from the Expo explaining Elias was just her neighbor?

"Can you talk about your job?" she asked, while searching for the restroom.

Elias gave a thoughtful hum. "Not really," he said apologetically. "I can tell you we focus on satellite surveillance, stuff like that, but that's about it. How about you?"

She didn't want to talk about *her* work. And there was the restroom where she could slip away to ascertain for herself if Stu had unfriended her. Did this mean he wasn't going to contact her tomorrow? A weight pressed down on her chest.

"I work for a taskforce that focuses on terrorism within a hundred-mile radius of the Capitol," she said breezily.

Elias's eyes glowed with interest. "Really. And that was your boss at the Expo," he recalled. "What's his name?"

"Ike Calhoun—actually, it's Isaac, but only his wife can call him that." An inner voice cautioned Hilary to close her mouth. While Elias obviously worked in the same line of business she did, they were in a public restaurant in Chinatown. Who knew what kind of listening devices were planted under the table capturing useable intel that could be analyzed by the Chinese to thwart the US?

"If you don't mind, I need to use the restroom," she said, pushing her chair back. "I'll be quick," she added, seeing his look of disappointment.

Once within the privacy of a toilet stall, Hilary opened Facebook on her phone and verified that, sure enough, Oscar Atta was no longer listed as one of her friends.

"Well!" She issued a huff of confusion, then wrestled with the concern that Stu hadn't believed her about Elias. Given her past reputation with men, she couldn't really blame him. Perhaps he wanted nothing to do with her. But that was silly. After all, Stu was the one who'd broken it off with her and broken her heart in the process.

Anyway, there was nothing she could do about it now that he'd unfriended her. She wanted to trust that his promise was still the strongest thing he valued. She wanted to believe he'd reach out to her tomorrow, but why cut her off? Again!

Sighing heavily, she put her phone away and finished her business. To have her hopes dashed when she'd been so pleased to have him back in her life was a cruel fate. How could Stu have done that to her? Tears of frustration stung her eyes.

She tried to tell herself it was for the best. If

Stu couldn't trust that she had really changed, he didn't deserve her. She would move on. She would find another man just like him. At least Elias seemed interested.

TWO HOURS LATER, Hilary slipped inside of her apartment, shutting the door between her and Elias. Only then did she wipe the taste of his kiss off from her lips.

Had she made a mistake agreeing to see him again, on Tuesday?

There'd been nothing inherently awful about his kiss. Elias hadn't been sloppy or clumsy. Like a gentleman, he had walked her to her door then stolen a gentle kiss—nothing that would explain her repugnance. With the excuse that she had to feed her cat, she'd turned the key in her lock and darted into her apartment.

Confusion stormed her. What was she supposed to do, dismiss the opportunity of a date in the hopes that Stu came through tomorrow, despite the fact that he'd unfriended her? He'd had all evening to contact her about his reasons for doing that, yet her phone remained conspicuously silent, like he hadn't believed her assertion that Elias was just her neighbor.

Well, screw him. She wasn't going to bank on him coming through at this late hour. By accepting Elias's request for another date, she'd at least ensured she wouldn't spend the entire week alone and miserable because Stu had pulled the plug on them. Again.

She was moving on, just as she'd promised herself she would.

"Mrreeow!"

Mitzie's yowling wrested Hilary from her misery. Somehow, some way, she would put Stuart Rudolph behind her.

CHAPTER SIX

O N SUNDAY MORNING, Stu stood in the chilly breezeway outside of Hilary's third-story apartment working up the nerve to knock. Someone nearby was cooking bacon, but with his stomach tied in knots, his mouth didn't even water.

He tried imagining Hilary's reaction to his unannounced visit. He hadn't warned her for a reason. If he surprised her in bed with her neighbor, he could still bow out of her life without telling her his number. Then he wouldn't be subjected to the kind of heart-wrenching messages she'd left him on his old phone. Nothing disturbed Stu like unbridled emotion.

Just knock, he ordered himself. He knew she

was home because her orange Mini was sitting out front in its parking space.

As he lifted his hand, it popped open without warning, startling him. There stood Hilary wearing curve-hugging black spandex, a pink windbreaker, and tennis shoes.

"Stu!" She gaped at him in evident amazement. "You're here."

He examined the statement from all angles, his hand still poised in mid-air until he remembered to drop it back to his side. "I said I'd reach out to you on Sunday," he reminded her.

"Yeah, but…You unfriended me on Facebook." There was no mistaking her accusatory tone.

"For a reason," he insisted. "We need to talk." His gaze returned to her tight-fitting attire. "Were you going somewhere?"

"For a walk through the park," she explained with a cool shrug. "I do it every day."

The park was a good place to talk. "I'll go with you."

She looked down at his lace-up loafers. "Can you walk in those?"

If he could run five miles in combat boots, carrying a sixty-pound pack, he could sure as hell walk in loafers. "Yup."

Another shrug. "Suit yourself." She pocketed her keys and pulled the door shut behind her. "Let's go."

They moved in what might have been tense silence down the stairs. It was sometimes hard for Stu to tell if the air was thick or not.

"This way." As they reached the parking lot, Hilary gestured with her head that they should head for the wooded area across the street from her apartment complex.

As they crossed the pavement, weaving their way through the cars, a sliding glass door rumbled open behind them. With instincts honed by years on the Teams, Stu looked back and up to see a man stepping out onto his second floor balcony.

Oh, shit was that…? Yes, it was.

Elias Malki froze with a coffee cup tipped to his face, but Stu still recognized him, and jealousy swamped him. He looked away and quickened his step, causing Hilary to trot to keep up.

A crosswalk conveyed them to a park of deciduous trees. When he slowed down, Hilary led them toward a path that curved under bright green leaves, then along a lake where they startled a flock of geese into the water. They had trekked a quarter mile or so in silence when Stu decided there wasn't any sense in putting off what he had to say.

"So your neighbor," he began, earning a sharp look. "I don't think you should be friends with him on Facebook."

She came to an abrupt halt, forcing him to back up and meet her flashing eyes.

"Why not? You really think I'm seeing him even though I told you I'm not?" Her tone conveyed anger and what he thought might be hurt.

His first instinct was to deny it, but truth be told he hadn't fully trusted her. "It's not that," he insisted.

"Uh-huh." Her cheeks flushed with emotions she kept to herself.

Stu tried again. "Elias has certain friends… Tarek Hayek and Sayid Zafrani. They're suspected ISIL supporters," he clarified when she just stared at him blankly.

A long silence followed his declaration, then she narrowed her eyes.

"Are you serious?"

"Of course." Stu didn't know why she asked that. Or why anyone ever asked that.

Her nostrils flared. "Stu, Elias works for the Intelligence Advanced Research Projects Activity. If anything, he's friends with ISIL supporters because he's monitoring their activity. Just like Oscar."

Possibly, but only a handful of agencies employed social engineering to manipulate extremists.

"Are you sure he works for IARPA?" His own research hadn't unearthed a shred of evidence that Elias Malki was employed by the government.

"Yes, I'm sure," she said. "He leaves the office at the same time I do. He practically follows me home."

Was that supposed to make him feel better? "Doesn't prove anything," he pointed out.

"Oh, come on." She notched her hands on her hips in a classic defensive posture. "He went to MIT. He was born and raised in Akron, Ohio. He speaks perfect American English. There's nothing remotely anti-American about his Facebook page. Maybe those friends you mentioned simply went to MIT with him. He is not a dissident," she insisted stoutly. "I know this for a fact."

"How?"

Her chin rose another inch. "Because he told me about his job. He also warned me not to be friends with Oscar Atta because *that man* is dangerous."

Stu felt the blood drain out of his head. It wasn't a good feeling. "Wait, my name came up?"

Hilary heaved a tedious sigh. "Yes. He asked me how I knew you. Apparently, he'd seen that we were friends on Facebook before you dumped me."

Her choice of words broke his train of thought. "Dumped you? I didn't dump you," he protested. "I should never have friended you from Oscar's account in the first place. That was a mistake."

If anything, his apology seemed to upset her even more. Instead of continuing to walk, she folded her arms across her chest and drew a shaky breath before speaking.

"Well, you and I aren't friends anymore—or should I say, Oscar and I?—so it doesn't really matter, does it? In fact," she stated, her voice growing tight, "I'm going on a date with Elias on Tuesday. I guess it's a little late, then, to tell me not to be friends with him."

Stu had to widen his stance to counteract the blow she'd just leveled at him. He spoke the first words to pop into his head. "You can't go out with him."

The sight of her delicate eyebrows winging upward informed him that wasn't what she wanted to hear.

"Watch me," she said through her teeth. Then she whipped around and marched away from him.

In four long strides, Stu caught up to her, grabbed her arm and pulled her around. "Wait. I said that all wrong."

"You have some nerve, you know that?" She cut him off, jerking her elbow out of his grasp. "You can't ignore me for five months then sweep back into my life and expect to pick up where we left off. I *loved* you." Tears glistened in her eyes like diamonds, putting a choke hold on his vocal chords. "You didn't say a *word* to me in five miserable months. You didn't answer any of my texts or voicemails. All you did was change your stupid number. So, guess what, Stuart? I've moved on. If I want to date my neighbor, then I will, and you can't tell me otherwise. And don't try to scare me away from him with some ridiculous allegations about terroristic activities. That's bullshit!"

With that final pronouncement, she took off a second time, stalking in the direction they'd come from and wiping her face as she went.

Stu had gotten the wind knocked out of him several times in the line of duty. It felt exactly like he was feeling right then. He couldn't breathe.

The only woman in the world he'd ever loved, aside from his mother and sisters, the only woman who'd ever understood him, was washing her hands of him because he was an idiot. He'd let stubbornness and, most recently, stupidity get in the way of keeping her close to him.

Shit! And now she was planning to go out with someone he suspected of holding radical beliefs, someone who was friends with terrorists.

Rousing from his dismay, he followed Hilary from a distance, keeping one eye on her while pondering how in hell he was going to get her back into his corner.

A voice in his head, sounding very much like his oldest brother Nick's, mocked him. *Stu, you are one stupid son of a bitch.*

AT THE POINT of returning to his balcony with a fresh cup of coffee, Elias stilled behind his sliding glass door, eyes widening at the sight of Hilary hustling back toward the apartments alone. Her pink nose, her pinched lips, made it obvious she was upset. Some distance behind her, Stuart Rudolph kept pace with a brooding expression.

Elias edged behind his hanging blinds so the man wouldn't see him again. Of course, Elias had recognized him right away as the GSG member they'd run into at the Expo. His instincts then—that Hilary had a thing for the man—were clearly right on target. Her being friends with a white-hat hacker was a source of serious concern. What if that man was astute enough to sense Elias's true intentions? Elias had been planning to use Hilary to get a camera into the National Counterterrorism Center. Beyond that, he'd been hoping for a long-term relationship with her. She was cute, smart, and sexy. He'd been confident of his ability to woo her, then eventually convert her to Islam.

Yet her present distress was plainly evident as she hustled back into their building. Perhaps Rudolph had broken her heart. Was that a good thing for Elias or a sign that her heart was already taken?

As she disappeared below him, Elias turned a thoughtful gaze on the source of her woe. Stuart Rudolph' plodded reluctantly toward his all-electric vehicle. As he stood there, indecisive about leaving, the door in the apartment above Elias thudded shut. With a look of resolution on his lean face, Rudolph took his phone from the clip on his belt and made a call.

Through the ceiling, Elias heard the faint chime of Hilary's cell phone. It rang and rang and rang, telling him she was refusing Rudolph's call.

Huh, Elias thought. Was it over between them? The tall man's shoulders sagged. He slowly put his phone away, got into his car, and after several minutes of just sitting there, drove away.

Good, Elias thought. The Ghost was gone, leaving Elias to his original plans. Yet, what if there was something better he could do? Rudolph and Hilary clearly had a connection, maybe even strong feelings for each other. In fact, Elias imagined that a well-timed phone call from Hilary would likely bring the Ghost running straight back to her.

Hmm. Excitement snaked through him as he considered the possibility of using that circumstance to his benefit. He pictured Sayid and Tarek's reaction. Imagine how impressed they'd be if Elias delivered a Ghost Security Group member to them on a platter!

Crossing toward his couch, he snatched up his worn copy of the *Qur'an* to inspire him. Leafing through it, he found the verses he was looking for.

"*Muster against them all the military strength and cavalry that you can afford,*" he murmured, "*so that you may strike terror into the hearts of the enemy of Allah.*"

Sinking onto his sofa with the book still open, he smiled with growing confidence. It was settled, then. He would use Hilary's relationship with Rudolph to lure that man to his death.

CHAPTER SEVEN

O N TUESDAY EVENING, at ten minutes to seven, Hilary dragged herself out of her apartment for her date with Elias.

"Just get it over with," she muttered as she locked her door and started for the stairwell. It was obvious she and Elias weren't going to end up in a relationship—not when her every waking thought was still of Stu. But she *had* to get over that damn SEAL. That damn sexy, smart SEAL. She sighed. Going out with someone else was the first necessary hurdle. She couldn't spend the rest of her life pining for a man who didn't know how to love her.

As her head cleared the third floor, she spotted Elias standing by his door waiting for her to join him. In contrast to the amber sky behind him, he struck her as especially swarthy, dressed in a maroon sweater and black slacks. His compelling gaze jumped up to intercept hers, but the smile she expected from him never came.

"You look great," he said, taking in the jade green dress and leopard-print heels with an intense regard.

"Thanks," she said while thinking her shoes sent the wrong message.

"Shall we?" Offering her his arm, he led her out into the parking lot. The burnished sun shimmered behind the branches of the trees in the park across the street.

"Do you mind driving?"

The unexpected question made Hilary blink.

"I'm having an issue with my car," Elias added, gesturing toward it as he marched them toward her Mini. "I need to take it to my mechanic tomorrow."

"Uh, okay." Hilary gave a shrug. "Sure, I can drive." She caught herself thinking she would have the option of ditching Elias in the middle of their date if she felt like it.

"Great." He walked her to her to car door, holding it while she slipped behind the wheel.

Then he rounded the vehicle and got in next to her.

The car seemed to fill with tension.

"Where to?" Hilary asked, turning up the heat as a sudden chill raised goosebumps on her arms.

"It's a surprise," Elias said rather shortly. "I'll give you directions. How's that?"

"OK." Hilary forced a laugh, while thinking longingly of her cat and her warm pajamas. Following Elias's instructions, she pulled away, heading toward the beltway.

"It feels like we're going to work," she commented as he guided them in the direction of McLean.

Apart from giving her directions, Elias kept quiet. Hilary cut a curious glance at him. He sat rigidly in her passenger seat, eyes glued to the four-lane highway before them. Where was the easy-going companion she had spent the other day with? How would they get through an entire dinner if he didn't relax?

"Does my driving make you nervous?" she inquired.

He swallowed visibly. "Well, you do drive a little fast," he said, causing her to slow her speed and move into the right lane.

"Sorry."

He said nothing in response to her bid to put him at ease. God help me, Hilary thought, snapping on the radio to ease the tension.

"Take the next exit," Elias ordered as they came up on the exit she took each day to work.

Hilary's curiosity simmered. As far as she was aware, there were no restaurants anywhere near the Liberty Crossing Intelligence Campus. "We're not going to your office, are we?"

"No." Elias's chuckle struck her as forced.

"Turn right?" They had come to the intersection where she'd first noticed him pulling up behind her car.

"Yes," he confirmed.

In her agitation, Hilary punched her accelerator as she came out of the turn. They were approaching the turn off toward the gate at NCTC when Elias reached into his front pocket and pulled out something shiny. A *snick* drew her gaze to the object clutched in his right hand. Before she'd even registered he was holding a knife, he leaned toward her, pressing the tip to her throat. As the sharp point broke the skin by her jugular, Hilary yelped, certain he'd drawn blood.

"Keep driving."

The steering wheel wobbled in her grasp. Oh, my God! He'd stuck her with a knife! Common sense ordered her to turn right toward NCTC, but her hope to avoid being sliced open overruled it.

"Watch the road," Elias barked.

The exit to the gatehouse came and went. She kicked herself for not driving straight to Harold, the guard, who would have rescued her. Too late now. She wanted to reach up and feel if blood was trickling down her skin, but Elias still held the knife to her neck so she kept her hands on the steering wheel, holding perfectly still. How could she not even feel where a moment ago he'd jabbed her?

"Wh-what—?" She couldn't even articulate her confusion.

"Do exactly what I say," Elias grated, his breath fanning her face, "or your cheek is next." The blade glinted at he moved it up near her right eye.

Hilary flinched from it. "What do you want?" she demanded.

"No talking. See the entrance coming up on

your left? Pull in there."

He wanted her to turn into a storage facility?

The unlit sign for **U-Store It** advertised se-cure and temperature-controlled units. She'd never even noticed the facility before, hidden as it was behind a chain-link fence trimmed with barbed wire. Compelled by the razor-sharp blade beside her cheek, she turned into the entrance, coming to a stop before the levered bar that blocked them.

"Roll your window down," Elias told her, "and swipe this card over the scanner."

Taking the card he gave her, she did as he said, only to regret not dropping it outside her car door. *Think, Hilary, think!* she railed at herself, even as Elias snatched the card back from her and the bar lifted.

Hilary cast a hopeful eye all around them. Perhaps another car would come along and someone would notice her being held at knife-point. But the area remained deserted.

"Pull in," Elias ordered.

No. Hilary was certain once she drove into this place, she stood little chance of ever coming out again. She had no idea what Elias wanted—whether he meant to rape her or sell her into the sex trade or what.

The tip of his knife touching her cheek forced her cooperation. She eased her foot off the brake and, of its own accord, her Mini rolled into the deserted enclosure.

With sudden insight, Hilary realized *this* was where Elias worked, not at IARPA. The facility was close enough to NCTC that he could see her vividly painted vehicle whenever she left the campus. He must have waited for her to leave each night then raced to catch up with her. My God, how long had he been planning this crazy abduction?

"Pull up to the back," he ordered, sounding more assured, perhaps due to being on familiar territory.

Her Mini coursed a narrow alley between the walls of two brick buildings.

"Turn right," Elias added as they reached the end at the back of the facility.

In the gathering gloom, the chain link fence on their left hemmed them in. Beyond the fence was a fire break, then nothing but trees. No one would see her when Elias dragged her out of her car into one of the rear units. Dread turned her limbs to lead and her mouth to dust. She thought of her phone, stashed in her purse, but that was sitting on the floor of the car behind his seat.

Suddenly someone stepped out of an unlit door—a uniformed security guard.

Hilary's hopes winged upward then crashed back to earth as she beheld the man's swarthy aspect and malicious expression. As he waved them closer, it was clear that he'd been expecting them. Was this one of Elias's friends—perhaps one of the dissidents Stu had mentioned?

Her heart wrenched with horror. Oh, dear God! Stu had been right about Elias, hadn't he? Elias was friends with terrorists. Worse than that, he was delivering her *to them*.

She braked, abruptly, refusing to go any farther. Elias reached over and killed the ignition. The other man's footsteps filled the sudden quiet as he stalked to her car and hauled her door open. As his rough hands seized her, Elias unfastened her seatbelt and reached for her purse.

To no avail, Hilary struggled. Every muscle in her body strained in protest as the stranger dragged her from her car then propelled her toward the door from which he'd emerged.

Unable to wrest free from the man's cruel grasp, Hilary found herself thrust into a short hallway, dark but for the light shining from one of a half-dozen rooms. The stranger shoved her through the open doorway, and she staggered into an enclosure roughly ten by ten feet. A naked lightbulb illuminated a third man, seated at a card table behind his laptop. The rest of the room was merely four bare walls and a cement slab for a floor.

At her entrance, the third man rose from one of two chairs to glower down at her. Tall and gaunt, with a beard that hid the lower half of his face, he struck Hilary as utterly ruthless. All oxygen left her lungs.

"Sit." He gestured to the second chair, which faced the table. She wasn't given an option or even the chance to comply. The second man pressed her down into it, while Elias shut the door, locking it with a twist of the deadbolt. *Clunk.*

Rocked by her thudding heart, Hilary swayed where she sat. Elias crossed the room, delivering her purse into the hands of the one who was clearly the leader. Without any respect for her personal property, that man pawed through her purse until he came up with her cell phone. He roused it, then regarded her with such soulless eyes that she felt her heart shrink.

"What's your password?" he asked, the soft tone of his voice causing a chill to race up her spine.

When she hesitated, he dropped her purse onto the table and approached her with a menacing swagger.

English, like Elias's, suggested he'd been born and raised in the USA. Hilary stared at him. She didn't keep any secrets on her phone, but she did keep contact information for her colleagues, including their street addresses. Holding her tongue, she quaked as she awaited the consequence of her silence.

With an impatient mutter, the man leaned down and seized her right wrist. Using his superior strength, he pressed her thumb to the scanner, and her phone immediately unlocked itself. Damn it. She had never considered that shortcut might be used against her.

"Next time you don't cooperate," he warned her, tossing her hand away, "Tarek will cut your thumb off."

Tarek? Her gaze jumped to the man by the door. Wait, she knew that name.

Tarek and Sayid. Stu's voice echoed in her head. Holy shit! Her supposition was correct. They *were* Elias's Facebook friends.

Shock dumped adrenaline into her bloodstream. Terrorists. She'd fallen into the hands of terrorists.

The leader, who had to be Sayid, was searching for something on her cell phone. He evidently found it, shooting a triumphant smirk at his companions. "He's here."

With that same cold smile on his lips, he started to compose what could only be a text— to whom? Was he texting Ike Calhoun? She remembered stupidly pointing him out to Elias. And if not her boss, then who?

In a flash of clarity, she realized the truth—it was Stu, who had introduced himself to Elias as a Ghost Security Group member, having no idea how much that title would intrigue Elias.

"Wh-what are you telling him?" she asked in a voice thin with fear.

Sayid glanced at his companions first, then shrugged and looked at her. "You know who we want?" he asked mildly.

She wet her dry lips in lieu of answering.

Sayid supplied the answer for her. "Stuart Rudolph. He's your boyfriend, right?"

She swallowed to find her voice. "No," she said truthfully.

Sayid ignored her. "Let's see how much he cares for you." He looked back at her phone and started texting.

Clearly, he meant to lure Stu to their location. "What are telling him?" she repeated.

"You'll see."

Sayid's upper lip disappeared into his mustache as he finished his text. Then, gesturing for Elias and Tarek to relax, he rounded the table and returned to his chair. He laid her cell phone next to his laptop, then dropped into his chair and folded his arms across his narrow chest.

"Now we wait," he added, gloating with the certainty that Stu would come to her rescue.

Hilary, who recalled with a pang how she'd rejected Stu on Sunday, was not so certain.

CHAPTER EIGHT

D RAGGING HIS GAZE from his watch, Stu
looked back at his laptop at Sayid Zafrani's latest Facebook post. It was hard to focus
on the cryptic message with thoughts of Hilary's
date interfering. He had nearly parked his car
close to her apartment that evening so he could
follow her and Malki on their outing. What if
the man mistreated her? What if she needed
rescuing?

In the end, he'd decided Hilary was smart
and feisty and, therefore, capable of looking out
for herself. Following her amounted to stalking,
so he'd returned to his hotel room after his
meeting with the Congressional Task Force on
Terrorism and Unconventional Warfare.

With his duty to Congress complete, he

could go back to Virginia Beach that night if he wanted to. But he didn't. He had walked away from Hilary the last time and had regretted it ever since. Leaving her with things the way they were between them didn't feel right. In fact, it felt plain awful.

By now, Hilary would have listened to the detailed voicemail he had left on Sunday, apologizing for his stupidity and begging her for a second chance. She had his new number; why wasn't she calling him?

Ugh! Now he knew how frustrated she must have felt all those months when he'd ignored her. It wasn't like he didn't deserve her cold shoulder. He did, but she was taking it a bit too far. For all he knew, she was on her date with Malki, which meant that Stu might never get her back. If only he could prove Elias didn't work for IARPA. That agency, unfortunately, laid claim to commendable security measures. Not even Stu, the Hacker, had managed to hack his way into its HR department.

Heaving a frustrated sigh, he looked back at Sayid Zafrani's latest Facebook post.

Tonight the Great Ghost faces Allah's judgment!

What the hell was that supposed to mean?

Stu analyzed the sentence word by word. *Great Ghost* called to mind the Great Satan, which was, of course, ISIL's favorite way of referencing the USA. But what if Ghost referred to Ghost Security Group; after all, members of GSG were referred to by the media as "ghosts." Why would Zafrani predict that a ghost would face Allah's judgment, that night of all nights?

The buzzing of Stu's cellphone kept him from theorizing an answer. His heart leaped to see Hilary's name accompanied by a text from her.

Hey, can you help me? I went to get a box out of storage and I got locked into my unit.

Stu blinked at the perplexing message before thumbing a quick reply: *Aren't you on a date right now?*

Her answer took almost a full minute. He was about to call her outright when she texted back: *No, I changed my mind. I went to my storage unit to get you something. The door closed behind me and I can't get out.*

Something for him? His jealousy cleared in an instant. Hot damn! She had changed her mind about Malki, and she was thinking about him instead! His heart seemed to expand in his chest. What's more, she was calling on him to be her knight in shining armor and rescue her from…a storage facility.

He glanced at his watch. 7:15 p.m. Couldn't she have waited until morning?

Impatient with texting, he jackknifed out of his chair and called her number directly. Her phone rang and rang, but she didn't pick up. Instead, she sent a map via text, pinpointing her location. Ironically, **U-Store It** appeared to be right up the street from the National Counterterrorism Center.

I want to talk to you, he texted her. *Call me.*

The reception is bad. We have to text.

Stu narrowed his eyes at the printed assertion.

The outside gate should open automatically, she added seconds later. *I'm in C3 in the back. I'll text you the code when you get here. Hurry!*

Stu scowled at his phone. Something—aside from the sheer bizarre nature of the request—felt off about out. True, Hilary was prone to doing the unexpected, but this was weird.

Querying the uneasy feeling in his gut, Stu thought of his friend and teammate Jeremiah, who'd taught him never to dismiss the whispers of his intuition. After all, Elias Malki was supposed to have been taking Hilary on a date tonight. What if Malki was somehow behind Hilary's bizarre request?

A sudden thought jerked Stu's gaze back to his open laptop and to Zafrani's mysterious post there: *Tonight the Great Ghost faces Allah's judgment!*

A suspicion pierced Stu's thoughts. Was it possible Elias Malki had enlisted Sayid Zafrani and Tarek Hayek in a scheme to lure and capture Stu of all people?

Raking his fingers through his hair, he sought a valid counter-argument. Zafrani and Hayek lived in Cambridge, Massachusetts, and Stu was down here. So how would they get their hands on him?

Easy. At Malki's behest, they could have hopped on a plane that morning. That man might have persuaded them they could use Hilary as bait to capture an actual Ghost Security Group member. Hell, they seemed pretty confident of their odds, enough to predict a victory on social media.

Certainty made Stu's scalp prickle. That wasn't Hilary texting him. It didn't sound anything like her. She was being used to lure him in.

What if he ignored her texts? The terrorists would likely kill her. He wasn't going to let that happen, and they knew it.

He needed help. Fast.

Stu's immediate instinct was to call up his teammates. With Tristan's ringer already sounding in his ear, Stu thought better of it and severed the call. Not only were his teammates several hours away, they were all involved in rigorous training that week and would never get permission from the CO to come to Stu's aid.

He turned and prowled the length of his hotel room. His thoughts went to Hilary's boss, Ike Calhoun, and he drew up short. The man had been a SEAL himself during the War in Afghanistan. When Tristan's fiancée had been shot in the head five months earlier, Calhoun had responded to a call for help, arrested the shooter, and promptly cleared the crime scene. As Hilary's boss and head of the Inter-Agency Counterterrorist Taskforce, he was the go-to guy.

Finding the man's contact information in his cellphone, Stu crossed to his suitcase as he placed the call. He accessed the secret panel at the bottom of his suitcase and withdrew the locked box that held his Sig Sauer Legion 226. Calhoun's phone rang four times before the man finally picked up.

Stu stammered through an introduction only to be cut off.

"I remember you. What's up?"

With the heartfelt hope that he wasn't wasting the man's time, Stu launched into a quick explanation of the date Hilary was supposed to be on with a man who had dissident friends on Facebook. Ike listened silently but intently.

When Stu finished with, "I think she's been abducted, and they're using her to try to get to me," Calhoun's chair gave an audible squeak. "She's texting me, telling me she locked herself in her storage unit, and she needs me to get her out."

"Who's her neighbor, and who are the dissidents?"

"Her neighbor is Elias Malki. He's friends with Sayid Zafrani and Tarek Hayek."

"Shit." Calhoun cursed on the other end, taking Stu by surprise.

"You've heard of them?" Stu guessed.

"Yes, I've heard of them. They flew into

Dulles this morning. We've been following them since, but they lost us around rush hour."

Stu's stomach lurched unpleasantly. *Too much of a coincidence.* "I think I know where they are." He strapped his paddle holster over his chest and cinched it tight.

"At the storage facility." Calhoun's voice was completely neutral, calm and commanding. "Give me the name."

"U-Store It. It's just up the street from NCTC."

"How the hell would they know about you?" Ike demanded. "Did Hilary tell them?"

"No, sir." Checking his magazine, Stu ascertained his pistol was loaded then slipped it into the paddle under his arm, along with two extra clips. "I ran into her and Malki at the Expo last weekend. Assuming the man had clearance, I introduced myself as a Ghost Security Group member. That's on me. They know what I do—or least half of it," he amended, thinking they still didn't know he was a SEAL.

"You're with GSG?" It was Calhoun's turn to be surprised.

"Yes, sir."

"Damn. Now it makes sense," Calhoun

murmured.

Stu immediately guessed he'd also seen Zaf-rani's Facebook post.

"Listen up," Calhoun added, his tone sud-denly more urgent. "Luckily, I'm at the office still, not far from her. Where are you now?"

Threading his arms through a lightweight jacket, Stu headed for the door. "Leaving my hotel in D.C." He zipped the jacket, concealing his weapon.

"Good. I'm assembling my team, and we'll meet you in my office at NCTC, second floor, third door on the right, as soon as you can get here. I'll clear you at the gate."

Relief eased the vice around Stu's chest.

"Yes, sir. I'm on my way," he said, scooping up his room key.

As the former SEAL hung up, Stu didn't even pause, texting Hillary's phone as he dashed down the corridor toward the hotel's exit: *Traffic is bad. I'll be there as soon as I can.*

Picturing her terrified by the wild-eyed ruffi-ans who were using her as bait, Stu's focus threatened to unravel. God forbid he never got the chance to tell Hilary how much she really meant to him.

He was slipping into his car thirty seconds later.

"SHIT!" SAYID THUMPED an open palm on the table, whipping Hilary's pulse into a gallop. He'd just received a text. Obviously from Stu and seemingly bad news.

"What's wrong?" Tarek looked up from the floor where he sat across from Elias, playing a game of cards.

Sayid's dark gaze lifted. "He says traffic is bad. He's keeping us waiting."

Elias riffled the cards in his hand. "Don't worry," he soothed. "He'll be here."

"How can you be sure?" Sayid shot back. "She says he's not her boyfriend."

"He loves her."

Elias's calm reply brought Hilary's head around. How could he be so certain? She and Stu had had a serious falling out at their last encounter. Her stomach cramped as she recalled her rejection of him, her stubborn refusal to believe her neighbor could be friends with terrorists. Yet Stu had been right about Elias all along, and she had been so wrong. Tears of remorse burned her eyes, but terror kept them from falling.

Sayid's laptop chimed, signaling an incoming post on Facebook. The sound distracted the leader briefly into reading whatever his followers might be saying to his latest comment. His eyes narrowed and then swung thoughtfully toward Hilary, whose nape prickled at his contemplative regard.

"Our brethren are asking for a taped execution," he announced to the other two.

Talons of fear clambered up Hilary's back and dug into her shoulders, stealing her breath.

Elias looked up sharply from the cards in his hand. "You can't post a video like that on Facebook," he cautioned. His gaze darted to Hilary, then back to Sayid, who shrugged off the warning.

"I'll find somewhere else to post it," Sayid said mildly.

Hilary's vision blurred as the blood drained from her head. *Taped execution?* She remembered Ike relaying a similar event that had nearly happened to his wife, Eryn, years ago.

Elias went quiet. When he spoke again, his voice came out on a strangled note. "Just the guy, right? Just Rudolph."

Sayid wrested his gaze from his computer to regard Elias. "What's it matter to you, Malki? You know we can't let her go."

"Yes, but..."

"Why would you care how she dies?"

Hilary's head seemed to fill with a fog. The voices of her captors came from a greater and greater distance.

All at once she felt herself falling. Her temple struck the concrete floor with a painful crack. The blow brought her sharply back to the moment, yet she kept her eyes intentionally closed, her breathing shallow. *Let them think I fainted.* Perhaps she could trick them later and rise up in retaliation—who knew?

All she was certain of was if Stu was caught and executed, his death videotaped and publicized worldwide letting ISIL crow in triumph, she would never, ever want to open her eyes again, even if she got the chance.

CHAPTER NINE

STU BURST INTO Calhoun's second-floor office a tad out of breath from his sprint down the last long hallway. Barreling through the empty secretary's alcove into the bigger office beyond, he came upon three men, all standing and looking at blueprints displayed on a wall-mounted monitor. Their heads swiveled at Stu's abrupt entrance.

"There you are." The silver-haired Taskforce leader beckoned him closer.

Stu noticed each man was wearing a Kevlar jacket, the sight of which jacked his heart rate another few beats per minute. They carried enough weapons on their bodies to start a small war. Meanwhile, Stu had been made to leave his Sig Sauer with security downstairs.

Calhoun made brief introductions. "Stuart Rudolph, meet Special Agents Jackson Maddox and TJ Hamilton."

Maddox was a light-skinned black man; Hamilton as tall as Stu, with a face that suggested American Indian heritage. Both men shook his hand, then they all looked back at the monitor.

"These are the floorplans to the storage facility," Calhoun explained. "Any idea what unit she's in?"

Stu scanned the plans in less than a second. "Right here. C3." He pointed it out while considering the facility's layout. "Her text said the main gate will open automatically. I'm assuming they'll have eyes on me and raise the gate remotely. Looks like I drive around back, through here." He traced the route with a finger. "I'm supposed to text her when I get there. I'm assuming the code is for the storage unit, and this door here will be unlocked."

"What if the code triggers an explosion?" Maddox's question betrayed first-hand experience with bombs and booby traps.

Stu's stomach lurched. He hadn't thought of that. Glancing around, he saw a laptop, open and active on the next desk.

"Can I use your computer for a moment?"

"Of course," Calhoun replied, looking curious.

Stu approached the keyboard, typed quickly as if someone's life depended upon it because he was now certain that it did, and then nodded at the info that appeared on the screen. He turned to the others. "It's unlikely the storage unit is wired. I just pinged Hilary's phone, and it's in the building. That means they're in there, too. They're not going to risk their own lives or risk triggering an alarm with an explosion."

Calhoun nodded, looking impressed. "Agreed. They want to capture Rudolph so they can pick his brain, not kill him right away."

"OK, so this is a basic rescue with one hostage and three or more unfriendlies," Hamilton stated matter-of-factly.

Stu swallowed. He'd participated in several HR missions, but he'd never been in love with the recovery target before. That circumstance made the whole scenario way more precarious in his opinion.

"What about cameras?" he asked, his voice gravelly with tension. "If they have eyes on the gate, we have to assume they're tapped into the rest of the surveillance system."

Calhoun stepped toward the monitor. "I just spoke with the company that installed it. It's a basic wireless system with remote access. I have a code that will override it. Once we're through the gate, I'll disable the system and they'll be blind."

Stu's respect for the Taskforce leader soared. An obvious question remained, however. "How are we all getting through the gate when they can see us?" he asked.

Calhoun pinned a bright green gaze on him. "What kind of car do you drive?" he asked.

"Nissan Leaf."

The man stared at him, his expression completely enigmatic, yet Stu had the feeling he didn't approve of his vehicular choice, especially in this instance.

"We're taking my truck," Calhoun informed the room at large. "Rudolph drives the Durango. The rest of us will be sitting in the back."

"But—" Stu remembered how Malki had been watching them from his balcony the other morning. "What if Malki knows that's not my car?"

Calhoun shrugged. "That's just a chance we'll have to take." Grabbing an extra Kevlar vest off the chair behind him, he lobbed it at Stu. "Put this on under your shirt," he instructed.

"HE'S HERE!"

Hilary nearly flinched at Sayid's sudden announcement. With her pulse racing, she forced herself to lie unmoving, even though the cement floor bruised her hip. Eyes closed, she continued to feign unconsciousness. After a brief discussion that revealed their original intent to tie her to the chair, the men let her be, assuming her to be unconscious.

Tarek and Elias abandoned their card game and scrambled off the floor. Hilary listened to them hurry over to the table. Peeking through her lashes, she saw them bending over Sayid's laptop, which apparently gave them a view of the front gate.

Her heart thudded painfully. She didn't know whether to weep for joy or in dread of what was about to happen. Hadn't Stu found her circumstances the least bit odd? Would a man with his training really stumble blindly into a trap like this?

"That's not his car."

At Elias's dark comment, Hilary snapped her eyes shut. The fear swirling in her gave way to hope.

"He drives a Nissan Leaf," Elias continued, "not a truck."

Stu must have guessed something was amiss!

"Is that him at the wheel?" Sayid demanded.

Elias took his sweet time answering. "Yeah, that's him."

Hilary fought to keep her breathing even.

"What the hell's in the back of that truck?" Sayid muttered.

"I can't see anything," Tarek answered. "The windows are tinted."

"Maybe he brought a truck because the text said she'd come to the storage to retrieve something," Elias suggested.

Sayid gave a growl of annoyance. "Tarek, stand over that bitch," he ordered.

With a lurch of her heart, Hilary realized she must have moved.

"If the Ghost tries anything funny, shoot her in the head but make sure he sees it."

Hilary's blood flash-froze. She listened to Tarek's approach, heard him flick off the safety on his pistol as if it was cannon fire in her ear.

"Wait." Elias protested unexpectedly. "Let me do that," he said. "I'm not equipped to take on Rudolph. You guys have the training, not me. I'll shoot her if he tries anything. You all worry about him."

"Fine," Sayid agreed.

Listening to Tarek and Elias trade places, Hilary wondered if she was any better off being shot by one man than the other. Maybe without training, Elias's aim would be off.

"Shit, now what?" Sayid hissed. His tone suggested something awful.

"Why aren't the camera's working?" Tarek asked.

"I don't know." Sayid tapped frantically at the keys. "Damn it. We've lost all visual contact. How is that possible?"

"Could he have overridden it?"

Oh, you bet he could, Hilary cheered inside her head.

"I don't know. Maybe. Go stand by the door," Sayid growled at Tarek. "We're proceeding with the plan. Maybe it's just a glitch."

Hilary could hear Elias breathing raggedly as he stood over her.

Her phone chimed, signaling an incoming text.

"What's it say?" Tarek demanded.

"He says he's at C3," Sayid answered, "and he's asking for the code."

"What do we do? Should we give it to him? What if we've been made?"

"Shut up," Sayid answered. "We stick with the plan. No more talking. I'm texting him the code." Two seconds of silence elapsed. "Turn out the light," he added.

As Tarek hit the switch, Hilary slit her eyes in time to see Sayid shut his laptop. The unit plunged into darkness.

Profound silence followed. Hilary strained her ears for the sound of Stu's approach.

This is it, she thought. The next few minutes would determine whether she lived or died. *I can't die!* She and Stu were meant to be together. Or, at least, they deserved the chance to figure that out. Her getting killed would accomplish nothing.

She made up her mind. She would not go down without a fight. Whatever it took to stay alive, she would do it.

OVER THE SOFT tread of his own soles, Stu heard the other three men steal up the unlit hallway behind him. His heart galloped like a thoroughbred. The cool deliberation he normally laid claim to during operations had utterly deserted him. His palms were actually sweating. *Get it together, man*, he told himself, even as his gut churned. If something happened to Hilary in the next few minutes, he would never forgive himself.

Each unit had been spray-painted with glow-in-the dark numbers. The number 3, halfway down the hall, beckoned him. Stu approached it while eyeing the glowing combination lock and recalling Maddox's concern that the code he'd been given could set off a detonation.

His mouth went dry at the thought. Not that he feared death. He just didn't want to die before making things right with Hilary.

The other three men were right behind him. Calhoun pressed his back to the wall on Stu's right side, while Maddox and Hamilton crept past him and plastered themselves to the wall on

Stu's left. When Calhoun tapped his shoulder, Stu applied his knuckles to the door as they'd discussed and called out, "Hilary? You in there?"

The silence that followed his query caused his fear to spike. What if they'd killed her already?

His phone buzzed as he received a text. "I'm here. Use the code."

Right. Like that was her.

At Calhoun's nod, Stu raised a hand and, with his breath held, punched in the four-number sequence. In lieu of exploding, the box gave a beep, and a click ensued as the lock released. Stu cautiously depressed the handle, then pushed the door open, just wide enough for Calhoun to toss a flash-bang into the dark interior.

As the metal canister skittered across the floor, a male voice issued a warning. A flurry of movement accompanied the explosion of noise and white light. Stu and company burst into the room. Calhoun swept left, firing as he identified a tango. *Thoop.* Maddox and Hamilton swept right. *Thoop.* Only two tangos were down, yet no one was left standing.

In the strobe of the flash bang, Stu recognized Hilary and Elias writhing on the ground. She was clawing and gouging him with all her might, fighting to relieve him of the gun in his hand.

For fear of striking the wrong person, Stu lowered his weapon. Either Maddox or Hamilton hit the light switch.

"It's not loaded!"

Elias's frightened cry penetrated Stu's consciousness. Glimpsing an opening, he dove into the fray and wrested the man's gun from his grasp and passed it off to Maddox, who checked the cartridge.

"Not loaded," he confirmed.

Prying Elias out of Hilary's ferocious grasp, Stu left him to Hamilton. He pulled Hilary gently upright.

"Stu!" She hugged him so fiercely she might have damaged a rib if he hadn't been wearing a Kevlar vest. As she quaked and shuddered against him, he drew her out of the chamber, away from the sight of dead bodies and of Hamilton cuffing Elias and reading him his rights.

Out in the dim hall, Stu had to put his back

to the wall to counter the sudden weakness in his knees. He kept Hilary locked against his chest.

"It's okay," he said, as much to himself as to her. "It's over." His heart continued to beat a loud tattoo.

For several seconds, she kept her face averted. When at last she looked up at him, the light from the room revealed that she had lost her glasses in the tussle. What's more, a lump had formed on her forehead, betraying that she'd been struck.

"They hit you?" He had to push the words through his suddenly tight jaw.

"No, I think I fainted." She even offered him a wry grimace to accompany her words. "One minute I was in the chair, the next, I was on the floor. Then I played dead."

While her answer reassured him, the tears rimming her lashes made him want to keep her in the citadel of his arms forever.

"Smart girl," he murmured.

"I'm sorry," she added, her face crumpling with remorse.

She was sorry?

"It's not your fault," he grated.

"Yes, it is." Twin tears raced down her cheeks simultaneously followed by more. "I was stupid and naïve. I'll never doubt you again, Stu. I should have listened. I—"

"I love you." He cut her off so she didn't beat him to it.

His confession had the desired effect of silencing her. A tremulous smile transformed her beloved face, chasing away her lament, and making every ounce of stress he'd endured perfectly worthwhile.

"Oh, Stu." She lifted her arms to catch his face between hands that still shook. "I love you, too, my beautiful, clever man. I was so afraid they would kill me before I got to tell you. I've been such an idiot."

"I'm the idiot," he insisted. "I should never have let you go in the first place."

"That's true." She issued a sound between a sob and a laugh. "You shouldn't have."

Calhoun stepped out of the door carrying Hilary's purse and glasses. He drew up short as he looked at them. "You two both good? Any injuries?" His tone betrayed surprise at seeing them looking so intimate.

Stu pushed himself off the wall. "No, sir."

With a smug smile Calhoun passed the items in his hands to Hilary, then looked her up and down as she put her glasses back on and visibly pulled herself together. "You okay, Hilary?"

She nodded rapidly but couldn't speak.

"You might want to have that bump on your head looked at," he added, proving there was little that escaped him. "I'm going to need to keep your phone," he added, apologetically. "I take it I can reach Hilary via yours, Rudolph?"

"Yes, sir."

The suggestion of a smile took years off Calhoun's craggy face. "Get the hell out of here," he ordered them mildly. "Just don't go too far. I'll need statements from you tomorrow."

As Stu drew Hilary toward the exit, Calhoun called out, "Hey, leave that vest in my truck."

"Yes, sir. Thank you, sir." Stu cast Calhoun a grateful backward glance. Pushing the door open, he swept Hilary outside into a sweet-smelling twilight and toward a future spent together.

CHAPTER TEN

S TANDING JUST INSIDE the door of Stu's hotel room, Hilary willed herself to shake off the memories of that evening. Even with Stu's arms firmly around her, the trembling that had taken hold following her rescue had yet to subside.

It was out of sympathy for her emotional state that Stu had agreed to forego the emergency room to have her head looked at. She hadn't wanted to be subjected to an MRI. All she needed was to be lulled into knowing she was safe again.

Stu had been astute enough to bring her to his hotel, in lieu of her apartment, where thoughts of Elias and how he'd duped her would keep her from relaxing.

"Let's get cleaned up," Stu suggested, leading her into toward the adjoining bathroom.

White shelves and dove-gray granite filled Hilary's peripheral vision as her gaze went straight to her reflection. The sight of her mussed hair and streaked makeup brought a whimper of dismay to her lips. Not to mention the bump on her forehead, which was starting to turn an ugly purple.

"You're beautiful," Stu assured her, apparently reading her thoughts. Then he frowned at her reflection. "What's that?"

Tipping her chin up, he peered at her neck while she watched him in the mirror, admiring the tilt of his dark head, scarcely able to comprehend that they'd both escaped such peril alive.

She immediately guessed what he was looking at. "That's where Elias pricked me with a knife to get me to keep driving."

"Bastard!" Stu exclaimed, releasing her with a possessive once-over. He reached decisively for the faucet and turned on the water. Grabbing a fluffy white washcloth from the neatly folded pile, he wet it, then tenderly dabbed at the dried blood, cleaning the wound with soap so it wouldn't fester.

A sudden urge to cleanse her entire body made Hilary declare, "I want a shower." She kicked off her leopard-print heels, which she couldn't believe had stayed on through her whole ordeal, and started peeling off her dress.

Stu took the cue to turn on the shower. With it running, he brushed her hands aside and continued to divest her of her outerwear.

Watching in the mirror, Hilary started to forget the evening's recent horrors. Stu laid her jade-green dress carefully atop the counter. Considering her practical bra and panties, he looked up at her with a rueful smile. They both knew if she'd known they would end up together that night, she wouldn't be wearing plain white cotton.

Brushing her spine with gentle fingers, Stu released the catch on her bra. When he slid the straps from her shoulders, she shivered. The bra fell away, exposing her generous, pink-tipped breasts. Stu drew an audible breath. Standing behind her, she could feel his erection through his slacks as he cupped her fullness then gently thumbed her nipples, causing them to flush and crown.

As pleasure arced low between her hips, Hilary let her head fall back on Stu's shoulder. Closing her eyes, she leaned into the solid wall of his body and offered her neck to him. The bristles on his jaw tickled her, raising gooseflesh on her thighs and forearms.

His large hands skimmed the hourglass curves of her body to divest her of her underwear. Wriggling free of it, she turned to face him, then tackled his own clothing with rising gusto. This was exactly what she needed to forget her brush with death. Under her deft fingers, his shirt came undone, revealing a crisp white T-shirt beneath.

He helped to discard the outer layers, revealing an expanse of taut muscle and smooth skin, lightly furred between his pecs. The muscles in his abdomen tensed as she stroked a trembling hand up his chest to run her fingers though the soft hair there.

"God, Stu, you look even better than I imagined," she murmured, putting her lips on one dusky nipple and tonguing the tiny firm peak.

Her hands tackled his belt with fervor. When she couldn't release it fast enough, he assisted her, jerking it open, then shucking his slacks and boxer briefs before she had the chance to remove them herself.

"In," he said, opening the shower curtain and indicating with a jerk of his head and a hungry glint in his dark eyes for her to step inside the steaming enclosure.

She did as he requested, wetting her body and tearing into the wrapped bar of soap in her eagerness to explore him. She managed to soap his broad chest before he wrested it away from her.

"This is about you," he said, rubbing the soap into the washcloth sitting in a tidy roll on the narrow shelf beside them.

He devoted the next five minutes to lathering every tense muscle in her body, from her neck and shoulders to her toes. By the time he straightened and quickly soaped himself, Hilary felt thoroughly cleansed. Her skin tingled and her muscles felt pliant. Through heavy lidded eyes, she drank in the sight of him, splendidly aroused with soap suds sliding down his thighs. In the next moment, she found herself sinking to her knees.

Stu muttered something in protest.

"I have to," she insisted. She needed to put

her lips on him, to taste him, to feel him filling her.

Steadying himself with a hand on the wall, and with a groan of surrender, Stu let her have her way, but not for long. Within a minute, he was pulling her to her feet and claiming her lips under his. She immediately coiled her arms around his water-slick shoulders and held on while he ravaged her mouth.

Desire stormed Hilary's arteries. Not a single memory of her recent horror surfaced to ruin the moment. Her eager hands coursed Stu's body, thrilling in every inch she touched, reveling in the feel of his possessive touch. Her mewls of wantonness blended with the patter of water in a duet of sensuality.

"I need you," she muttered against his chest. "I need you now."

"We should go to the bedroom," he offered, but then his fingers slid into the slippery spot between her thighs, and she knew he was as eager as she was.

Gasping, she lifted one foot to the edge of the tub to give him access. Rocking her hips, Hilary showed him what pleased her. He slid two fingers inside of her, answering her silent plea for more.

"Stu!" Her nails dug into his shoulders, and she welcomed his fervent stroking.

But it wasn't enough. She needed him to claim her for his own. Once she was his, the last vestiges of fear still clinging to her would dissipate like water down the drain.

"Take me now," she begged against his lips, her voice a husky whisper. "Take me right here."

He didn't argue. With a determined expression, he backed her against the cool tiles, hooked his arms around her upper thighs, and lifted her. Hilary coiled her legs around his hips, securing her hold on him. The head of his sex teased her opening, making her want to sob with desire.

"Please, Stu," she cried, gripping his shoulders with helpless wanting.

By way of an answer, he filled her with his tumescence, covered her mouth with his, and surged his tongue between her parted lips to mimic the dance of their hips.

The sensation of him filling her, filling her to completion, of knowing it was Stu—finally, at long last—was beyond anything Hilary had ever felt before. Her rapture overflowed, first in rivulets and then, as the rhythm of his powerful thrusts increased, in a current that impelled her toward a shattering climax.

The walls of the steamy chamber echoed with her cry of ecstasy. With a groan of fervent agreement, he buried his face in her hair and shuddered, again and again, nearly losing his grip on her as his climax shook him.

They both seemed to melt. Hilary's back slid down the wall until her feet touched the bottom of the tub. Stu sank forward, pinning her between himself and the warmed tiles. They shared the same oxygen. Their lips brushed and lingered as aftershocks of their pleasure sparked over them like fireflies.

Reaching out with a long arm, Stu twisted the faucet to turn the shower off.

In the quiet that followed, the only sound was that of their heavy breathing and the tub draining. Gazing deeply into the bottomless depths of Stuart Rudolph's chocolate-colored eyes, Hilary acknowledged that a new chapter of her life had just begun.

"I love you," she murmured, stroking the slick wet hair at the nape of his neck.

For the longest time, he looked at her, his gaze touching on her lips, her breasts, the bump on her head.

"Marry me," he said, unexpectedly.

Hilary gaped at him. Perhaps, with his special mind, Stu didn't realize this wasn't necessarily the best time for a proposal. She had nearly been killed today. They were standing naked in a bathtub, for heaven's sake!

"Umm." She licked a droplet of water off her upper lip.

He straightened with a look of dawning alarm. "Did I say the wrong thing?" he asked on a note of genuine concern.

"No." Her impulse was to reassure him. "It was perfect," she soothed. True, she had always pictured a typical proposal with the man down on one knee, ring glinting in a velvet-lined box. She doubted Stu had anything like that on hand, but the question had come from his heart, unpracticed and genuine, and that was reward enough.

"Yes," she said, and the confidence in her voice reassured her. "I will."

A smile of wonder lit his face.

"I'd be honored," she added, pressing a kiss

to his lips. That answer, she had to admit, was one that she'd rehearsed. But Stu didn't need to know that.

OTHER BOOKS BY

MARLISS MELTON

ECHO PLATOON SERIES
LOOK AGAIN (Novella #1, permanently free)
DANGER CLOSE
HARD LANDING
FRIENDLY FIRE
NEVER FORGET (short novel)
HOT TARGET
TAKE COVER, a novella

TASKFORCE SERIES
THE PROTECTOR
THE GUARDIAN
THE ENFORCER

NAVY SEAL TEAM 12 SERIES
FORGET ME NOT
IN THE DARK
TIME TO RUN
NEXT TO DIE
CODE OF SILENCE, a novella
TOO FAR GONE
LONG GONE, a novella
SHOW NO FEAR